Sea Otter Inlet

CELIA GODKIN

Fitzhenry & Whiteside

This book is dedicated
to you dear reader

Sea Otter Inlet

Fitzhenry & Whiteside
195 Allstate Parkway
Markham, Ontario L3R 4T8

Acknowledgments:
The author wishes to thank Jane Watson
for graciously giving of her time and counsel.

Canadian Cataloguing in Publication Data

Godkin, Celia
    Sea otter inlet

ISBN 1-55041-080-6

1. Sea otter - Juvenile literature. 2. Kelp bed ecology –
Juvenile literature.. I. Title.

QL737.C25G62 1997   j599.765'5   C97–931809–2

Sea Otter Inlet

CELIA GODKIN

Fitzhenry & Whiteside

In a long arm of the sea,
hemmed in by land on either side,
lived a colony of sea otters.

The sea otters lived their whole lives
in the waters of this inlet.
They dived in the deep
seaweedy forests of kelp,
looking for good things to eat.
They dined on crabs and shellfish,
on sea stars and octopi,
but their favorite food of all
was the spiny purple sea urchin.

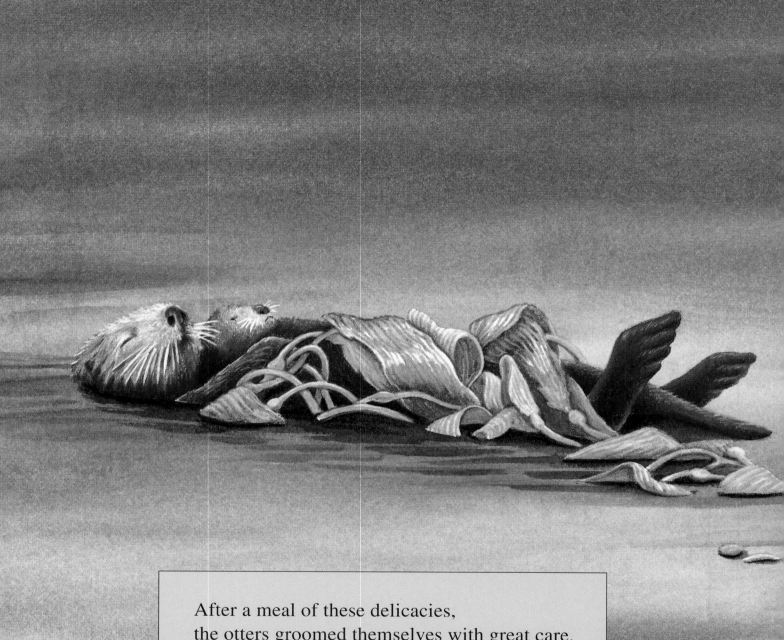

After a meal of these delicacies,
the otters groomed themselves with great care.
When they were as clean as they could be,
they wrapped themselves in a frond of kelp
and went to sleep.
The kelp anchored them gently in place
so they could not drift away.

One day the otters awoke from their nap
to find hunters all around.
The hunters hurled harpoons at them
or shot them with guns.

The otters dived to escape the hunters.
But they could not stay below the water for ever.
The hunters waited patiently
for the otters to come up for air.

One by one,
the otters were hunted and killed
for their soft, warm fur.
When there were no more otters left,
the hunters sailed away,
and life in the kelp forest went on.

There were clingfish
clinging to the flat, leaf-like blades of the kelp.
There were kelpfish eating the clingfish.
There were sea bass eating the kelpfish.
And there were many more fishes,
too numerous to mention,
swimming in and out of the kelp forest.

The kelp forest was made of giant seaweeds
with flat leaf-like blades
attached to a long, flexible stem.
The stem went way way down
into the watery depths
and attached at the bottom
to a firm piece of rock.
The attachment – called a holdfast –
anchored the kelp plant
so it would not float away.

Living on the bottom,
on and around the kelp holdfasts,
were all kinds of shellfish.
Some lived in cupped shells.
Some lived in coiled shells, like snails.
And some lived in shells
made of two halves hinged together.

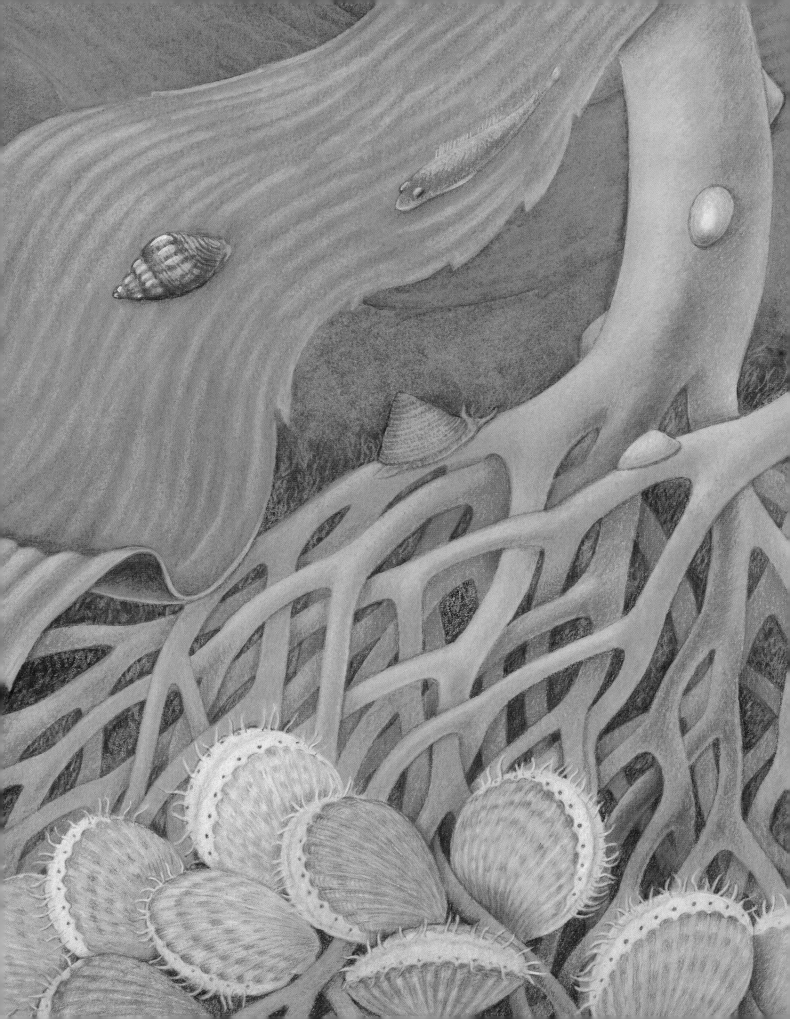

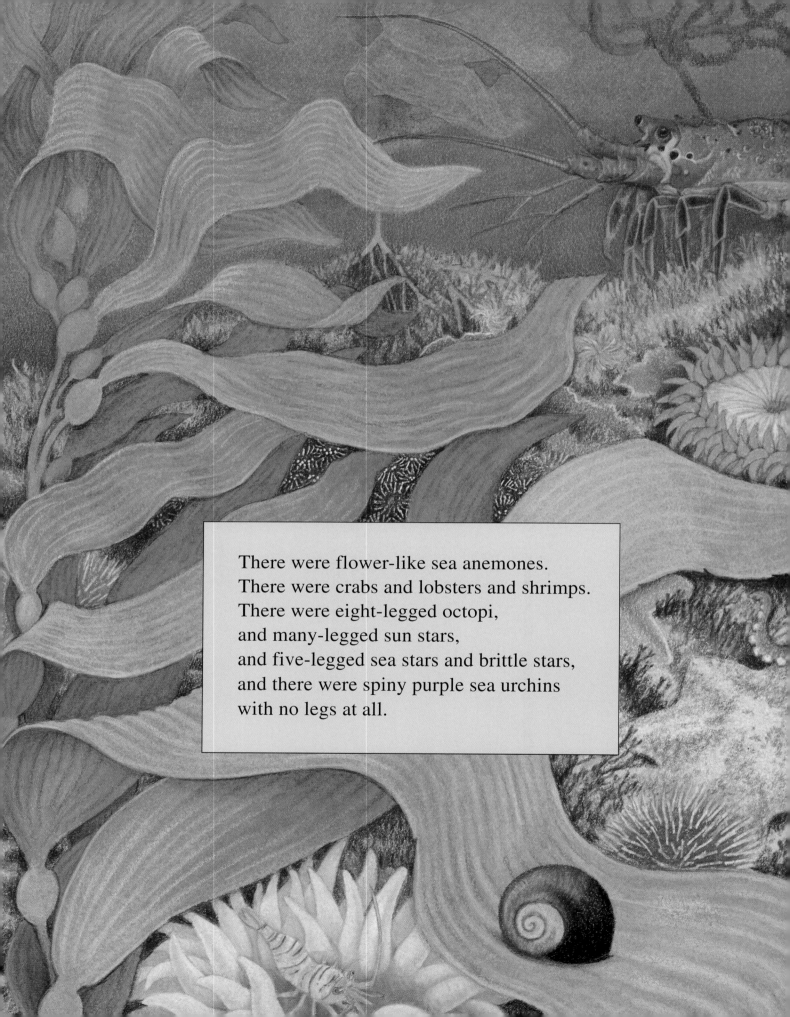

There were flower-like sea anemones.
There were crabs and lobsters and shrimps.
There were eight-legged octopi,
and many-legged sun stars,
and five-legged sea stars and brittle stars,
and there were spiny purple sea urchins
with no legs at all.

For a long, long time,
life in the kelp forest went on
much as it always had done.
Except that there were no sea otters
collecting crabs and shellfish,
or sea stars and octopi,
and there were no sea otters
collecting their favorite food;
the spiny purple sea urchin.

Without the sea otter to eat them,
the spiny purple sea urchins began to multiply.

The spiny purple sea urchins
multiplied and multiplied.
Soon there was an army of them
marching across the forest floor.
The spiny purple sea urchins
ate all the kelp holdfasts in their path.
The kelp plants had nothing to anchor them,
and floated away.
The animals that lived in the kelp
floated away too.

The kelp washed ashore and rotted on the beaches.
The animals washed ashore too
and died in the hot sun.

Those animals that lived on the bottom,
under the kelp, had no place to hide.
Other animals, living outside the kelp forest,
came in to eat them.

The army of spiny purple sea urchins
moved across the forest floor.
The kelp forest drifted away.
The animals that had found shelter there
drifted away too, or stayed and were eaten.

Then, one day, a wonderful thing happened.
Some sea otters swam into the inlet.

Some otters had survived in places
which the hunters had not found.
No one was hunting them anymore.
There were now enough otters
that some could come back
to live again in their old home.

The otters dived in the waters of the inlet.
They found plenty of spiny purple sea urchins.
Their favorite food!
Soon, other otters joined them.

Gradually, very gradually,
as the otters ate more and more
spiny purple sea urchins,
the kelp began to grow back again.
Gradually, very gradually, the animals
that had lived in the kelp forest returned.

Once again, there were clingfish
and kelpfish and sea bass,
and many more fishes,
too numerous to mention.

There were all kinds of shellfish.
There were flower-like sea anemones,
and crabs and lobsters and shrimps.
There were eight-legged octopi
and many-legged sun stars
and five-legged sea stars and brittle stars.

There were even
some spiny purple sea urchins,
with no legs at all.
But not too many.